Copyright © 2008 by Margaret Chamberlain
All rights reserved

CIP Data is available.

Published in the United States 2008 by Dutton Children's Books
A division of Penguin Young Readers Group
345 Hudson Street, New York, New York 10014
www.penguin.com/youngreaders

Originally published in Great Britain 2008 by Hodder Children's Books
A division of Hachette Children's Books.
An Hachette Livre UK Company.

Hodder Children's Books
338 Euston Road
London NW1 3BH

Printed in China
First American Edition
ISBN 978-0-525-47982-6
2 4 6 8 10 9 7 5 3 1

Please Don't Tease Tootsie

Margaret Chamberlain

Dutton Children's Books

PLEASE

don't tease
Tootsie,

or provoke
Poochie.

Don't madden
Mutley,

... or disturb Dixie.

Do not bully Bitsy,

or even think
of tickling Trixie.

You'd be NUTS

to wind up Whitney.

Just give her
a little pat...

...and PAMPER

Dixie cat.

Mutley's here for you
to dote on.
Will you put his new
blue coat on?

How about
a green newt sweet?

It's Bitsy's day
for bunny fun,

so MAKE THE EFFORT

EVERYONE!

Calm down,
Poochie.
It's all right.

Poor Tootsie!
Pretty Tootsie!
Come and curl up
on your mat.

We will stroke you,
never poke you.

We love you,
TOOTSIE CAT!